KENT ISLAND MYSTERIES

CAPTAIN BOYLE'S TREASURE

A NOVEL BY MARK L. LIDINSKY

First published by Dog Ear Publishing
4010 W. 86th Street, Ste H
Indianapolis, IN 46268
www.dogearpublishing.net

ISBN: 978-1-4575-1166-0

This book is printed on acid-free paper.

Printed in the United States of America

Foreword

THIS HISTORICAL NOVEL IS SET ON BEAUTIFUL KENT ISLAND LOCATED ON MARYLAND'S EASTERN SHORE. AS A YOUNG BOY FROM BALTIMORE, MY FAMILY AND I CROSSED THE BAY BRIDGE MANY TIMES HEADING EASTWARD FOR OCEAN CITY, MARYLAND. NOT ONCE DID I REALIZE THAT THE LAND AT THE END OF THIS LONG BRIDGE WAS AN ISLAND.

NOR DID I KNOW THAT, AFTER JAMESTOWN AND PLYMOUTH ROCK, KENT ISLAND WAS THE THIRD PERMANENT ENGLISH SETTLEMENT IN THE NEW WORLD. WE'D JUST STOP FOR ICE CREAM AND ASK HOW LONG IT WAS TO "O.C."

FOR FIVE YEARS NOW I HAVE HAD THE PRIVILEGE TO LIVE ON THIS MAJESTIC ISLAND, STUDY ITS RICH HERITAGE, AND MEET MANY OF ITS WONDERFUL PEOPLE WHO HAVE BECOME FRIENDS. KENT ISLAND IS NO LONGER A "STOPOVER", BUT A CHERISHED AND LOVED DESTINATION.

MUCH OF THIS NOVEL INVOLVES REAL PLACES ON THE ISLAND THAT EXIST TODAY. SOME ARE IMAGINARY. MOST OF THE PRESENT-DAY CHARACTERS ARE FICTIONAL BUT MANY OF MY FELLOW

ISLANDERS WILL RECOGNIZE SOME POSSIBLE COMPOSITES. ANY SIMILARITIES ARE NOT BY DESIGN.

CAPTAIN THOMAS BOYLE WAS A REAL IRISHMAN FROM MARBLEHEAD, MASSACHUSETTS WHO LEFT HIS MARK AS A BRAVE SEA CAPTAIN DURING THE WAR OF 1812. HIS EXPLOITS COMMANDING THE BALTIMORE-BUILT *CHASSEUR* ARE DOCUMENTED. HE TRULY MADE HER THE "PRIDE OF BALTIMORE" AND HIMSELF A HERO IN THE WAR OF 1812.

AS WE PROUDLY CELEBRATE THE 200TH ANNIVERSARY OF THAT WAR, PLEASE ENJOY SOME HISTORICAL FICTION SET ON THE LARGEST ISLAND OF THE CHESAPEAKE BAY. WHEN CAPTAIN JOHN SMITH WAS MAPPING THE AREA IN THE EARLY 1600s HE WROTE THAT "HEAVEN AND EARTH NEVER AGREED BETTER TO FRAME A PLACE FOR MAN'S HABITATION."

WE RECENT MARYLANDERS GREW UP CALLING THIS PARADISE "THE LAND OF PLEASANT LIVING" (FROM AN OLD *NATIONAL BOHEMIAN BEER* COMMERCIAL). IT TRULY IS.

MARK L. LIDINSKY
KENT ISLAND, MARYLAND
MARCH 17, 2012

Taylor Day - Kent Island High School (Class of 2012)

In the United States, every possible encouragement should be given to privateering in time of war...

By licensing private armed vessels, the whole naval force of the nation is truly brought to bear on the foe...

While the contest lasts, that it may have the speedier termination, let every individual contribute his mite, in the best way he can, to distress and harass the enemy and compel him to peace.

Thomas Jefferson on *Privateers*
July 4ᵗʰ, 1812

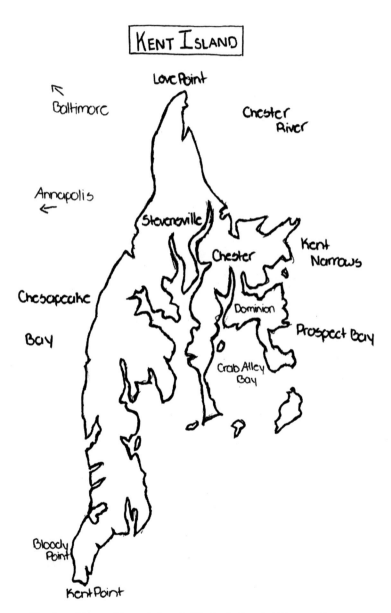

Taylor Day - Kent Island High School *(Class of 2012)*

Chapter One

It was yet another busy Saturday in the sweet-smelling bakery. This October day before the "Eve of All Hallows," 2013, people lined up to buy their favorite pastries. One young lady was seated in a corner, creating her special wedding cake, while a seasoned citizen asked when he could order his Thanksgiving and Christmas pies, and the November chill was still far off!

The PEACE OF CAKE was Kent Island's hidden treasure, an old-fashioned, make-it-from-scratch, bakery nestled in historic Stevensville. It was so legendary that people from across the Chesapeake Bay, Annapolis and the Western Shore, braved the dreaded Bay Bridge to snare its delights. Year after year the "Best Bakery Awards" easily went to this corner hideaway.

The three young ladies behind the counter were covered in flour and icing, leaning over their new delicacies. Oldies radio belted out Tommy Tutone's "867-5309...Jenny I got your number."

Megan needed additional sugar and headed to the back room. The old cupboard shelf was always too high for her. As she went up the stepladder and grabbed the sideboard, flour, sugar and coloring crocks came crashing down, as did Megan. The rusty hinges ripped ancient painted wallpaper and wooden slats from the wallboard surface; then she saw it.

After assuring the others that all was "OK," Megan gently removed an old leather satchel embedded beneath the yellow-white plaster. What was this – maybe old paper money or coins? There was a local legend that some bandits may have lived here in the 1940s. Megan unwrapped the frayed cords and found a tattered parchment that was torn on one side. After a few seconds, she realized she was holding some kind of partial map, written in quill-like ink style and dated "1815." At the very bottom there was a signature: "Captain Thomas Boyle...good ship *Chasseur*."

Megan Shockley was twenty-four and grew up on Kent Island. She knew that this piece of map she held in her flour-covered hands was a crude rendition of the largest island in the Chesapeake. There was the Chester River and there Love Point. This was a hand-drawn map of her home, Maryland's own "Isle of Kent." But it appeared she only had the left or North side. She put the map in the satchel, placed it in the wooden table drawer, and went back to help eager customers. This could wait.

Shannon O'Hare - Kent Island High School *(Class of 2013)*

Chapter Two

Some background history on Megan's mystery map maker...

As early as December, 1812 the British had declared a naval blockade of the Chesapeake and the Delaware Bays. As far as navies go, this was worse than David and Goliath. Even though George Washington and the American colonists had sent the Brits packing and a new nation had been established, the arrogant "Limies" wanted to teach the new United States a lesson. There were numerous issues including the former colonists' involvement in Canadian affairs. The U.S. was also accused of trading with Britain's sworn enemy, the French. America was not prepared.

In June of 1812, President James Madison was forced to declare war because 'The Greatest Naval Power on Earth' captured American ships at will, took cargo and even pressed sailors to serve in the British navy against their will. Madison had courage, since the Brits sailed over 600 warships and the United States a mighty sixteen vessels!

The only way to overcome these odds was to allow *any* American ship to attack and seize *any* British ship. Madison issued what were called "Letters of Marque and Reprisal." The Americans now sailed private boats that were also armed raiders. They were termed 'Privateers.'

Ship builders from Baltimore created the famous Baltimore Clippers, ocean schooners that could out-sail any British warship, and the tide turned. Eventually, American Privateers would capture or sink over 1,700 enemy ships.

This is where Captain Thomas Boyle and his *Chasseur* sailed into history. The man was bold and had extreme valor. Outside the British Isles in 1814 he declared his own blockade of all enemy vessels. He even sent an official notice to be posted in London!

In subsequent sorties, Boyle sank or captured eighteen British ships. It was patriotic *and* profitable. Boyle would put his own men on some of the vessels and sail them back to the United States. These, along with their cargo, were sold at auction and owners, investors, Captain, and crew divided the spoils according to custom.

When the War ended in 1815 with the *Treaty of Ghent*, the good Commander sailed back to Baltimore in April. The people of Baltimore had valiantly repulsed the British (who had just burned Washington) in September of 1814, and Boyle returned a conquering hero. He fired a salute to Fort McHenry where the future National Anthem was inspired. The very swift *Chasseur* was built at Fells Point, and citizens lined the docks and declared her the justified 'Pride of Baltimore.'

However, before turning his port side into the Patapsco River and Baltimore, apparently Boyle had made a nocturnal stop on an ironically British named Isle just before the Patapsco, Kent Island. Now, almost two centuries later, evidence of his 1815 clandestine visit was surfacing, and other wars would begin - treasure wars.

Chapter Three

AGNUM DOCKS was started by an enterprising former teacher from Queen Anne's High School in 1989. He gave up the terrible fluorescent lighting for the 'real rays' and began constructing docks and bulkheads all over Kent Island. Mack Robinson and his handyman, Knott, were very good at what they did. They installed the beautiful decks and moorings at locations like the BRIDGES RESTAURANT on the Kent Narrows. Every day they fought the tides, the foul weather, and angry customers who wanted the job completed yesterday.

Mack sat atop his red backhoe, smoking his pipe non-stop, and barking orders to Knott as they began a new bulkhead project on Queen Anne's Drive in Chester. While Mack perched high and dry in his blue denim shirt, poor Knott was in waders with mud and saltwater everywhere. The last bucket dumped the usual rocks, oyster shells and dirt, but something clanged amid the rubble. Knott grabbed an old cracker tin and tossed it aside. He liked collecting odd things that they dug up.

That night, back home in Bayside, a part of Stevensville, Knott ate the dinner he had picked up from IT'S THE PITS, baby-back ribs and coleslaw, all washed down with a bottle of the local beer nectar, National Boh. He mused how Mack had lectured him one day that it was "National

Bohemian Beer", not "Natty Boh" as some Hollywood bloke called it on the old TV series *Homicide*. Once a teacher...always a teacher!

Knott turned his attention to the now-dried find that he had placed in an ACME plastic bag. It took a good five minutes to pry the lid off the old *Maryland Cracker* tin. Inside, wrapped in coarse cloth, was what appeared to be an antique brass compass. It looked like it still worked. On the back were the initials "T.B." and "1813."

Chapter Four

Some additional Island history...

Kent Island was first inhabited by Native American Indians. In 1631 a Virginia trader named Clairborne established a permanent trading post on the southern point of the island. Eventually he lost his claim, both in England and through local skirmishes in the 'New World' to the Calverts. Their colony of Maryland was founded in 1634 and Kent Island would become part of Maryland – not Virginia.

The island would survive the Revolutionary War, the War of 1812, the Civil War, and all subsequent wars. After World War I there was a serious attempt to turn Kent Island into a bombing target for the Navy. The good local citizens, led by State Senator James Kirwan, went to Washington *en masse* and won the fight to have this rejected.

Every book written about Kent Island discusses its natural beauty, the rugged watermen (oyster, clamming, fishing and crabbing done expertly by many), and the extensive farming on its rich soil. And almost every book laments the one thing that changed Kent Island forever, the building of the Bay Bridge.

For many islanders, July 30, 1952 was their day of infamy. To add insult to injury, the two-lane WILLIAM

PRESTON LANE, JR. BRIDGE was followed up by a parallel three-lane bridge in 1973! The old ferry boats carrying people and a few cars were one thing, this was now an invasion.

Many longed for the 'good old days' when the island was isolated from mass construction, fast food joints, and incessant traffic. By 1990 the preservationists had made inroads to stop the sprawl. Key pockets of Kent Island were to be kept pristine, and watermen and farmers could pass down their cherished heritage. Crab traps and corn fields now coexist with CHIC-FIL-A and K-MART in an uneasy truce. However, this was certainly not the tree-lined, almost deserted island that Captain Boyle beached his long boat on back in 1815.

Chapter Five

$\mathfrak{M}$issy Biscuit was the titular head of the Kent Island Heritage Society (KIHS). She diligently catalogued all written and oral traditions of the island she loved. At ninety years of age, Missy was the prototype of Santa's 'Mrs. Claus' and she still drove her maroon Buick every day – some said better than most teens.

Every May, Missy and her historian friends at the KIHS dressed up in period costume and celebrated "Kent Island Days" in Stevensville. It was a fun reminder that history is an integral piece of life, especially for those living on the Chesapeake Bay islands.

The theme of 2013's May celebration was ironically the War of 1812. For a few weeks in August, 1813, the British had occupied a small eastern strip of land on Kent Island, just where the Narrows merges into the Chester River. They also established camps at Broad Creek, Parson's Point, and Kent Point. Belleview Plantation, Blue Bay Farm, on the northwest side of the island became their field headquarters. The Brits loved raiding the farmhouses for food, and here they had found paradise. There was a skirmish at Slippery Hill near Queenstown, technically off the island, and raids on St. Michaels, but no real battles. The British ships left in late August, some say 'highly encouraged' by the local mosquitoes.

Missy was well-known for her occasional history lectures and her expertise in the KIHS section of the library, but she was better respected as a premier baker. Her black walnut cakes were legendary. The girls at PEACE OF CAKE wanted this recipe badly, they had tasted it for years at the Kent Island Days bake sale which Missy supervised. After numerous requests and downright begging, the girls had persuaded Mrs. Biscuit to share her secrets. There was one condition – PEACE OF CAKE would donate additional goodies to the homeless shelter of Kent Island. All agreed. Thus fate would bring Missy and Megan face to face over black walnut cake.

"And don't use that fake butter – use the real thing…and rich whole milk," Missy insisted.

Megan had taken detailed notes at the store's table and was about to thank Mrs. Biscuit when she remembered to ask her, "Aren't you the person who knows all the history about our island?"

Missy took off her reading glasses and informed Megan of her role at the Kent Island Heritage Society. Megan excused herself, went to the back room of the bakery, retrieved the old leather pouch, and showed the contents to Missy. After adjusting her glasses and studying the document, the seasoned baker removed them yet again and gazed into space. All she could mutter was, "Oh, my!"

Chapter Six

Since she was a young girl, Mrs. Biscuit had heard rumors of buried treasure on Kent Island. In the 1880s there was an influx of 'diggers' who claimed pirates had planted gold and booty. They insisted they had old maps to prove it. All amounted to nothing but fun and frustration.

Now it appeared Missy was holding in her hands a piece of 19th century history involving her Kent Island and possibly one of the most famous characters of the War of 1812! This was half a map, but it had crude instructions of a starting point, compass directions, and definitive coastlines of the northern part of the island.

Thomas Boyle, she remembered, in the truest sense of the word, was indeed an American patriot. He was also a privateer and, in some ways, a pirate. Was this proof that the old rumors about buried booty were true? Missy and Megan forgot everything about black walnut cakes as their imaginations turned to history and possible treasure.

Chapter Seven

There are truly good people in the world but, unfortunately, some just as bad. Horace Alex Jeter was a giant in the land of the latter. Horace appeared on Kent Island in the spring of 1995. The Maryland Historical Society was issuing state grants to deserving groups who would investigate aspects of Maryland's heritage and document lost sites and artifacts.

Somehow Horace Jeter convinced the Historical Board that he had information on the possible location of the original fortifications established by the trader Clairborne in the early 1600s on Kent Island. His 'research' was as bogus as his history degree from Michigan State, but he somehow received one of the grants. Jeter's real motivation was to sell anything he could uncover on the black market for his own profit. History was a means to his nefarious ends.

Yet for three summers, Horace supervised college and graduate students in various sites around Bloody Point on the southern tip of the island. There are numerous theories on the name "Bloody Point" but no one is certain of the nomenclature. One of the nicest dig finds was a mug that dated from the 17th century. Horace would log in the discoveries and wait until the students departed at summer's end. Then he would sell whatever he could, documenting just enough Indian head arrow tips and shards of pottery to seem legitimate. On the black market he found a buyer who paid $3,000 for the mug. Each summer it was the same scam until funds ran out in 1998, and all summer projects ceased.

However, the biggest find that final year was what a student stumbled across under some rocks. It was a weather-worn leather pouch that contained a partial map of what appeared to be the southern area of Kent Island, north up to Matapeake. Jeter sensed the potential importance of this map, congratulated the student from Loyola College in Baltimore, and by September destroyed all recorded logs of its existence. There were odd markings and compass readings, and Horace thought it might be a treasure map. He did not care about its historical importance. This would be his alone and not go on the black market.

Chapter Eight

In 1998 'Professor' Jeter (he actually called himself this) moved to Kent Island and settled into the town of Dominion. The old map was the motivating factor. Over the years Dominion had a rough and tumble reputation and until the early 1900s was called "Devil's Dominion."

Horace ran an unlicensed construction company, specializing in what he called 'historical restorations.' He helped on projects like the Kirwan House in Chester, all the while looking for objects to secretly stow in his truck. He joined the Kent Island Volunteer Fire Department for two short years, and, for appearance sake, became a member of the Kent Island Heritage Society. Most of his time he searched high and low for anything old he could sell – after telling the owners it was junk. He even sold stolen things on E-Bay.

Horace's real obsession was the partial map he lifted from the digs. He studied the markings and old compass readings and swore that one day it would lead him to some sort of treasure. Time and time again, Jeter would set out with a small backhoe attached to his dented blue Ford pickup, usually by moonlight, and dig up any grounds that he thought significant from the map. Half of a map might reveal something...

Mounds of dirt were found all over the southern part of the island – on farms, beaches, abandoned house lots and even some parks. The local Sheriff deputies at first thought someone was burying bodies or illegal fish catches but only discovered dug up earth and tire tracks. This was a lot of effort for a prank. When yet another call would come in to headquarters, about twice a month, they knew the 'night digger' was at it again. They were frustrated, then embarrassed, and eventually angry.

Horace never was caught and never became discouraged. Casually, he would bring up the subject of buried treasure to some members in the Heritage Society, and there was amused laughter. He dared not show his map to anyone; legally he'd have a lot of questions to answer. He really believed the laughs were on these historical skeptics. His evening searches would continue.

Chapter Nine
A Diversionary Tale's Beginning

How exactly did the map of Captain Thomas Boyle get torn in two and his compass placed into a cracker tin? Why were these items on Kent Island to begin with? Most importantly, was a real treasure buried there in 1815? Some of these queries have answers; some do not. A diversionary tale must be told at this juncture to explain some of the mystery.

The Emma Giles

Shannon O'Hare - Kent Island High School *(Class of 2013)*

The *Emma Giles* was one of the majestic steamships that emerged on the Chesapeake decades after the Civil War. In March, 1887, she was christened in Baltimore by her namesake, Emma Giles, the five year old daughter of one of the owners, E. Walter Giles. By 1920 the seasoned steamship made regular runs from Baltimore's Light Street Dock to places like Tolchester, Eastern Bay, and many small communities up and down the Chesapeake.

Before the advent of cars and trucks, boats like the *Emma Giles* were the backbone of commerce and passenger transportation. The *Emma* was a 'day boat.' Other steamships had cabins for overnight runs. These wonderful ships would leave Baltimore daily with manufactured goods and equipment, along with many passengers anxious to get out of the big city, if only for an excursion on the Bay. They would return from places like Taylor's Island and South River loaded with freight of watermelons, oysters, and crabs. The rural passengers would be anxious to get to the big city and shop at large department stores like HUTZLERS in downtown Baltimore.

What started out as a sunny and humid August morning in 1920 soon turned into a vicious squall as the beautiful

The Love Point Hotel
1890-1947

Shannon O'Hare - Kent Island High School *(Class of 2013)*

Emma Giles steamed into the Chesapeake from the Patapsco River. Captain Michael Connor knew he would have rough going to his destination at Eastern Bay; he had grounded boats many times in less turbulent seas, so he quickly changed course for safe haven at Love Point on Kent Island.

Two seasick passengers, (sister and brother) Sarah and Jake Muth had had enough. They debarked, got rooms at the LOVE POINT HOTEL and, without wishing it, became main operatives in the lost treasure of Captain Thomas Boyle.

Chapter Ten
A Diversionary Tale's Middle

The Muth family was quite rich from iron business investments and had their estate just outside of Chicago. After World War I the parents, erudite philanthropists, spent most of their time in Europe.

Sarah and Jake, ages nineteen and seventeen, were dispatched to Baltimore to visit relatives and explore the Chesapeake as part of their education. After two days of listening to their boring Aunt Patsy and her sycophant husband Bill, they said a hasty goodbye and set out on their own. The breakfast of hot dogs and eggs was the last straw.

Kent Island was such fun that they stayed for three days: renting sail boats on the Chester River, fishing for rock fish on chartered boats, and just exploring the quiet island villages and towns. The seafood and fried chicken were exquisite.

By day three the sky was again overcast. Jake suggested a fun way to pass the time before their departure the next morning. He had read about this in *Harpers Magazine*: "Bury your own Time Capsule!" Serious Sarah declared the project stupid, but over scrapple and eggs at breakfast, Jake convinced her that it was a sort of bond they would share for the future.

Jake was the sentimentalist and knew that many of their rich friends' families had dissolved over money and disagreements. In his own way he wanted to cement their sibling care for each other by any means. It was simple: take two objects each that he would provide, hide them on Kent Island, and agree to return twenty years later and see if they were still here. Both would promise to bring back their future families in 1940. *Harpers* said local governments and people all over the USA were doing it to commemorate "The War to End All Wars." As it was too cold to swim, Sarah reluctantly agreed.

As the skies got darker, Jake appeared on the hotel's long wooden porch with two leather satchels and two cracker tins. Sarah opened them up and discovered a piece of scrimshaw, an ancient brass compass, and two pieces of an old parchment that looked like it was torn in two.

"What's this junk? Where did you get it?" she asked.

Jake explained that a local shopkeeper in Stevensville sold him a small trunk of nautical things for three dollars. Besides these items, there were other old documents, brass buttons, and a broken spyglass. Jake agreed that they were worthless but perfect for their little game. He was unknowingly somewhat mistaken.

The rest is simple history. Jake took his role seriously, rented a buggy, and headed south as he wanted to see the lower island anyway. He buried the satchel near a place called Bloody Point under a pile of rocks. He etched an "X" on the nearest oak tree. On his return, he rode eastward and found the town of Chester, at one time called Sharktown. By a small bay he hid the tin with the compass near a farm called Marling. On the closest tree he carved out another "X."

Sarah was far less ambitious. She hid the tin with the scrimshaw in the carriage barn of the hotel. She then travelled to Stevensville to buy some gloves. On one street she noticed some construction work of a back addition on a corner house. As rain drops began to fall, she slid the satchel with the partial map between small wooden slats and covered it with additional wood. How she ever thought she could retrieve this in 1940 was beyond comprehension, but at least she finished playing the game she deemed stupid. By Labor Day, 1920, the siblings were back in the Windy City and living their lives through the 'roaring' decade.

Chapter Eleven
A Diversionary Tale's End

Some mysteries remain mysteries. No one will ever know who brought the nautical items to the Stevensville shopkeeper. Perhaps it was an illiterate soul in need of fast cash who found them while removing trees or plowing the earth for harvest. The biggest shame rests with the shopkeeper. He bought the chest for a measly dollar and turned it on an unsuspecting tourist for three dollars.

"These idiot visitors from the steamships will buy anything old, even the fake maps I sell by the dozens!" he mused.

He allowed possible *real* treasure to slip through his greedy hands.

Another huge mystery is why Captain Boyle did not take his map and compass with him. Security? Fear of questions from authorities about his unscheduled stop? By all accounts, the patriotic pirate lived in Baltimore for a short period after 1815 and supposedly died at sea in 1825. It appears he never returned to Kent Island.

Nor did the Muth siblings. Sarah married a horse breeder from Colorado and devoted much time to establishing a women's soccer presence in the US. She lived to see the first Women's World Cup in 1991. Jake started a baseball bat company, Big Barrel Bats, and made a huge fortune.

Their parents had lost everything in the 1929 stock market crash, and the family seldom saw each other except at weddings and funerals. 1940 passed and promises made on the porch of the LOVE POINT HOTEL were never kept.

It would take some sort of "pirate miracle" to bring all of Boyle's treasure clues together again. Some two hundred years after his visit, would his ghost come back to orchestrate his unfinished business?

Chapter Twelve

rima Nix, the "First Snow", came on November 20th for Kent Island. It was a light dusting, but the wind was howling this Monday before Thanksgiving, 2013. Tonight the Kent Island Heritage Society scheduled its years' end meeting and banquet at the Kent Island Yacht Club at the Narrows.

Missy Biscuit's little speech as archivist was to summarize this year's topic on the War of 1812 and inform everyone where additional reading materials could be found in the library. She decided to spice up the pre-Christmas gathering with a little surprise. Without telling the President of the KIHS, Tom Kreamer, she invited Megan to come and reveal to the members her historical find. This would allow everyone to eventually study the half map and confirm her suspicions that it was indeed real. It could engage debate and study for years. Forget about boring Kent Island 'occupations' by the British in 1813, this was *huge* historical news! Missy loved surprises, and this was a blockbuster.

Megan had called Mrs. Biscuit and offered to pick her up due to the weather. She refused and stated, "Just bring the satchel in a good plastic cover, and meet me at the club. And don't show it to anyone. If people ask, you are my guest."

As Megan drove on Rt. 50 East, the Mama's and Papa's were singing in perfect harmony on the radio: "Go where you wanna go...do what you wanna do..." Megan was doing neither tonight. This gathering of people was certainly not her element. Sure, she probably casually knew some from THE PEACE OF CAKE, but to address a group of the KIHS! At Kent Island High School she almost always failed history. Missy told her that tonight would be easy; just tell how you discovered the partial map and hold it up. Missy would do the rest. Megan still had butterflies and was definitely nervous.

Chapter Thirteen

om Kreamer was a distinguished looking man in his mid sixties who had been a pilot for US Airways. He called the meeting to order, and all sat down to the crab cake or chicken dinner. Ninety-nine percent took the crab cakes, but consensus was they needed a little more OLD BAY seasoning. The biggest announcement that evening was that the bar was 'open' courtesy of BAKER'S LIQUORS. This was the first 'open bar' in the history of the KIHS! The women all wore nice winter outfits, and the men ties and jackets – the Planning Committee insisted on proper holiday decorum.

Even before the salads were served, some noticed that one individual had already made at least four visits to the bar. He was dressed in old brown pants, a wrinkled blue shirt, faded corduroy jacket and no tie. Yes, a scrubby-faced Horace Jeter decided to come tonight. Very few really knew him, since he naturally only showed at KIHS gatherings when food was involved. His signature rudeness continued when he asked the lady next to him if she was going to finish her second crab cake, if not, he would gladly help.

By now the light dusting was turning into a heavy snowfall, so Kreamer would move things along. He asked Missy if she could begin her talk early during dessert. Megan and Missy had both noticed the SMITH ISLAND CAKES and both simultaneously declared them "Super Market-made" as they laughed.

As President Kreamer quickly finished some agenda items, he introduced, "the woman who needs no introduction, Missy Biscuit." A buzz settled over the forty-some society members as Missy, with a young, pretty and unknown girl, approached the podium. Some speculated that it was sweet of Missy to bring her granddaughter to this stodgy party.

Chapter Fourteen

Missy completed her remarks in less than two minutes. Coffee cups and silverware clanged as she then announced, "And finally, I have a pre-Christmas surprise for the KIHS that may have great historical significance for Kent Island."

She introduced Megan and asked the wait staff to stop clearing tables so she could be heard. From President Kreamer to the newest member of the KIHS, Dennis Mahoney, a retired history professor from the University of Notre Dame, all paused and were a bit perplexed.

Megan told her brief story of the clumsy discovery and her discussion with Mrs. Biscuit. As she held up the satchel and gingerly brought out the parchment, the room went even more quiet. She read the inscription at the bottom. At this point, Missy joined her at the podium and declared, "I have every reason to believe that this document was written by *the* Captain Thomas Boyle in 1815, and it is a partial map of our Kent Island. We welcome input from everyone and know that this will provide KIHS discussions for years to come - if it is authentic."

Dead silence gave way to a few claps and then sustained applause from the entire group. No one noticed that the weasel-like, little man with no tie had just spilled coffee into his lap.

Despite Kreamer's admonition to watch the snow and drive safely, everyone wanted to get a quick glance at the parchment. Missy proudly stood by the plastic covered document like a Swiss Guard at the Vatican. Professor Mahoney explained to a few people exactly who Captain Thomas Boyle was and his importance in the War of 1812. Kreamer asked Missy why the 'surprise', and she just smiled. Megan quietly drifted into the bar area.

As Horace Jeter approached, a napkin covering his lap, he tried not to allow his eyes to bulge out of their sockets. He said nothing but immediately knew this was the other half of his stolen map. Same texture, same ink...and it showed the northern part of Kent Island! He stared long enough to see compass readings that were not on his document. In his heart he plotted historical robbery and mused, "Thank you, Mrs. Biscuit, for the 'Christmas Surprise!' Have you ever heard of the Grinch?"

Unfortunately, for the Planning Committee, tonight most people left without checking their bids on the silent auction due to the surprise and the inclement weather.

Chapter Fifteen

As cars and SUVs pulled out of the club, the snow was now two inches deep and falling steadily. Jeter warmed up his rusty Ford truck and believed one of four people would take the document with them: Mrs. Biscuit, President Kreamer, the document specialist, Paula Peddicord, or that bakery girl, Megan, from PEACE OF CAKE. Jeter did not want copies made and distributed just in case this side of the map revealed more than his. One would think that you needed *both* sides, but he was unsure. The sooner he stole it, the better.

Megan said her goodbyes and drove home to her condo near LOWE'S NURSERY in Stevensville. Peddicord went home to feed her two dogs, Molly and Maggie, in Chester. A misguided proponent of the global warming hoax, she looked at the early snow and declared it "climate change" to keep the myth going. An excited President Kreamer found his way slowly to his farm near Bloody Point. It was Missy who clutched the satchel closely and drove gingerly through the flakes home to Marling Farms. She had indeed spiced up the KIHS dinner!

Since visibility was now close to zero, Jeter could not tell who had the document. He sized up these four candidates in his mind and decided that he could wait a bit. He would request a viewing under the guise of historical research; it had worked on the digs years ago.

So tonight Jeter would celebrate. How ironic that he chose the NO PLACE bar in Stevensville. This was a notorious Pittsburg Steelers watering hole across the street from PEACE OF CAKE. He drank until closing, went home to Dominion, and dreamed of becoming a successful stealer.

Chapter Sixteen

The Wednesday before Thanksgiving, Missy deposited the satchel and map in the old safe used by the KIHS in the Stevensville library. Megan had entrusted it to her for safe keeping. She didn't bother to tell anyone, even Mrs. Peddicord, because, to her knowledge, no one else knew the ancient combination. All her attention turned to stuffing turkey and homemade pie preparations.

By now Jeter was going a bit crazy. He blatantly called Mrs. Peddicord's home phone and inquired when historians could view the found map shown at the banquet. She replied that she had no idea and referred him to Tom Kreamer. When she asked who he was, he hung up his cell-phone.

Each day that went by was now sheer torture for Horace. That same Wednesday, he even went by PEACE OF CAKE and walked into the buzz saw of people picking up their Thanksgiving pies. He spied Megan but knew she couldn't talk. He got close enough to say, "Congratulations on your discovery." Megan thought this really odd and just nodded at the disheveled man. These delays were killing Horace Jeter.

Tom Kreamer called Missy around 2:00 pm and said he had a big favor to ask. She cleaned her hands of wet turkey stuffing and listened. The year-end KIHS newsletter was coming out on December 8th; could she write a short article on the find and let people know they could view it in the new year? Kreamer wanted the press for the KIHS. "This is how historical funding goes to some places and not others. Why not get an early jump for interest in Kent Island?" he inquired.

Missy was not happy with the time restraints, but finally agreed. "And Happy Thanksgiving, Tom!" she said and hung up her now ancient 'princess' phone.

Chapter Seventeen

The day originally established by Abraham Lincoln to give thanks came and went. By December 5th, Jeter was getting extremely desperate. He drove to the Stevensville library and was told they knew nothing about a map discovery. It had to be with Kreamer, Mrs. Biscuit, or this Megan girl. He decided to target Missy's house first. For a few days he watched her leave around lunchtime and return around 3:00pm. He did not know she played Canasta with friends almost daily.

On the 6th he went around the back of her house at 1:00pm after Missy departed; there was nothing but corn fields behind the quaint, gray structure. He easily broke into her garage, forcing in the side door to the kitchen. For forty-five minutes he searched every closet, drawer and bookshelf but found no satchel. When the police arrived around 4:30pm, they kept asking if anything was stolen. Missy had not entered her home when she saw the lock busted but stayed with her neighbors, Jenn and Matt. She and her sons could find nothing of value missing; jewelry, petty cash and antiques were all there. The same day new locks were installed, and Missy's grandson, Nicholas, stayed with her for a week. No one connected the map find with the break-in. Jeter was apoplectic with rage. Peddicord at the library and Mrs. Biscuit were off the list for now.

Chapter Eighteen

The KIHS Newsletter arrived at members' homes by December 10th. No pictures were attached to Missy's article. She gave all the credit to Megan and ended with the generality, "In the new year we invite historians and anyone interested to examine the parchment by appointment. Contact the KIHS."

Kreamer was happy. Once there was confirmation of its validity, he would enjoy telling the world.

Two key people read the article that evening – one with curiosity, the other with dread. Now, for certain, Jeter did not want to wait until the new year. What if some idiot historian found a treasure location just through this portion of the map; he had to have it immediately!

The curiosity was provided by the dock builder, Mack Robinson. When his helper, Knott, showed him the old compass weeks ago, he was mildly amused. As a passive member of the KIHS, Mack read their newsletter to see if any potential jobs might come his way - as they did on the Kirwin House boat landing project. He remembered the "T.B.", "1813" and started connecting things in his mind. Mack never attended any KIHS functions, but he did know Tom Kreamer. Tomorrow he would ask Knott to bring the antique compass to work. The date of "1813" and the initials "T.B." were too much of a coincidence. When they finished some pile driving the next day, Knott let him borrow the compass.

Chapter Nineteen

An evening meeting was hastily set on December 12th at the Kent Island Library. Tom Kreamer invited Missy, Megan, Knott, and Robinson. By now Missy and Kreamer were mystified. Not only a parchment but a real artifact could be in play! Boyle's ghost was moving fast.

Kreamer decided to jump the gun on the new year timetable plan and also invited noted historian Kam Browne from the University of Maryland at College Park. Professor Browne was an expert on the War of 1812 in the Chesapeake. Her famous book, Maryland War Pirates, had become the definitive work on privateers from this period.

Missy slowly turned the combination of the safe as the small gathering fingered the brass compass; Knott took all the credit for salvaging the cracker tin. After twenty minutes of thorough examination of parchment and compass, Browne smiled at the diverse group and said only, "Congratulations!" She explained that this was indeed a 'personal' map with readings and notations pointing to a specific location. More study was required, but she felt that the other portion of the map was probably needed. Browne was more than excited that the famous Captain Thomas Boyle might have been on Kent Island. So little was known of Boyle after the War of 1812, that this find was of utmost importance for historians.

Missy and Kreamer envisioned historical headlines, while Knott and Megan wondered if they hit a potential treasure lottery. Mack Robinson, usually unruffled, was so excited that he had to go outside and fire up his pipe. For the time being the map and compass would be kept in the safe, and all agreed to convene again in January.

Unfortunately, too many people now knew too much. Despite President Kreamer's admonition to, "Let's keep this strictly to ourselves for the holidays," that was probably not going to happen on Kent Island.

Chapter Twenty

By the 13th of December, Jeter could wait no longer and called Tom Kreamer directly. His rapid-fire conversation went like this, "Tom, you probably know that I was in charge of the historical digs down on Bloody Point in the 90s. Saw the map at the Yacht Club banquet and read Mrs. Biscuit's article. Would sure like to get a closer look at the find as soon as possible. Where exactly is it?"

Tom was not sure to whom he was talking on his cell. Who was Horace Jeter? What digs on Bloody Point? He vaguely recalled a "Jeter" on the KIHS membership lists. Kreamer was busy that day and did not want to violate his own 'keep it to ourselves' advice, so he politely told this Mr. Jeter to contact him in the new year, as Missy's article stated. Horace was persistent and would not hang up.

To get rid of this pest, Kreamer mistakenly uttered, "The finds are in the safe custody of the KIHS, like all other important documents, and it's way too much trouble to get to them for the holidays."

Jeter disingenuously uttered, "Merry Christmas" and hung up. Finds??? Other important documents??? Kreamer had led him back to the Kent Island Library.

Late the evening of the 13th, Jeter made his boldest move yet. Fortified with some *Yuengling* drafts from the local

RAMS HEAD tavern, he drove directly across the street and parked his Ford on the far side of the library.

It was a very cold night. As he snuck up to a side entrance, some Canadian geese flying overhead startled him. It took five minutes to ascertain that there were no alarms. In two more minutes he broke the rusted lock. Jeter forced two inner doors open and found the Historical Room used by the KIHS. After ransacking the shelves and drawers, he cursed when he discovered the old safe. Foiled again by a bunch of amateur historians! He simmered in silent angst.

Chapter Twenty-one

The break-in at the library was big news in this small community. Nothing taken...nothing really destroyed. It sounded too familiar to Missy Biscuit. On the 14th she asked for a quick meeting with Kreamer, Megan, and Peddicord. Someone was targeting the KIHS and one of its oldest members.

Over coffee at HOLLY'S RESTAURANT, Peddicord related the strange phone call she received regarding the map. She also thought it queer that another librarian was approached, and a man had asked to see the new 'historical find.' Megan told of her weird conversation with an odd man at the PEACE OF CAKE. Missy was now convinced that the break-in at her home was too similar to the library incident – nothing robbed.

Kreamer now knew enough from yesterday's phone call to him to connect the dots. This man Horace Jeter could be the link. There was not enough proof but plenty of suspicion. Was this all the work of one individual? Was it Jeter? No one else expressed such urgent interest in the parchment. What to do now? And all over a historical map? It didn't make sense unless something valuable was involved.

Chapter Twenty-two

The local sheriff, Andy Costello, did not like break-ins on his island. He was just elected on "tough on crimes" promises in early November, and now there were two disturbances back-to-back. His office still had a black eye over the 'night digger' problem. His opponent, Will Dukes, even had people carry shovels at poll locations as a sign of chagrin. Costello won by only fifty votes. And now this...

On December 15th the sheriff listened intently to Kreamer and Missy Biscuit as they explained everything they knew to him. Kreamer said that he researched the 1990 digs at Bloody Point, and those who remembered him had no real praise of Jeter. Some called him "shady." Costello thought all this talk was quite a stretch; you can't accuse someone over historical curiosity. Everything they said was circumstantial. He said the department would keep an eye on this man Jeter, but he refused to go any further.

As the sheriff's car left Kreamer's house, Missy was frustrated and began to develop her own plan of action. Now she knew why she voted for the other candidate, Will Dukes! There had to be something important for all this attention to a piece of parchment. Maybe Professor Browne was right about a specific personal location on the map.

Maybe someone smelled treasure and was willing to do anything to get at it.

She explained her trap to a curious Kreamer and noted that Megan and Knott had to agree to go along. They would especially need Kam Browne and her expertise. Kreamer had to protect the KIHS; he was aboard. If they were wrong about this Jeter fellow, no harm would be done. So, on this noted fishing island, they would cast some irresistible bait lines and see what fish they landed.

Chapter Twenty-three

A mild front came over Queen Anne's County on December 20th with highs well in to the 50's. Horace Jeter checked his cell phone messages at 10:00am and could not believe his ears. It was Tom Kreamer asking him to attend a special gathering of interested people due to recent developments regarding the new map parchment. As "someone who knew Kent Island history through his research and digs," would he like to attend? The time: 8:00pm on the 21st at PEACE OF CAKE – the site of the find. Select others would also be there. Jeter was intrigued and salivating with greed.

Around the baking prep table sat Megan, Kreamer, Missy, and Kam Browne. Tom had cleared things with Knott and Robinson. Their presence would be overkill. Tea, coffee and cookies were already served when Jeter knocked on the front door at 7:55pm. Megan immediately recognized the man as the creep who approached her the day before Thanksgiving.

Kreamer introduced everyone, and the game plan concocted by Missy began. He stated that he wanted to meet before the new year because he feared someone was targeting the map find. He layered it on thickly as he explained in detail. If this small group agreed on its real value, he would take extra precautions and rent a safe deposit box the next morning – with Megan's and Knott's permission. Did the group think the document was worth that additional expense? Why was it so important?

The President argued that the two break-ins were enough evidence for him, but what did the others think? Browne played her role perfectly, pretending to be a novice to the map situation. As she declared its authenticity yet again, she also addressed the importance of the compass. Jeter could not believe that Thomas Boyle's compass was also found, and he fondled the brass to death as he studied the map.

With his best game-face, Jeter claimed he was unaware of the robberies but agreed wholeheartedly with Kreamer that "historical things had to be protected." This from black-market Jeter! The fish was circling the hook. He then uttered something stupid, "From my extensive research of Kent Island, I agree with Ms. Browne that these artifacts look authentic. Let's take extreme caution to protect them for the sake of history."

Missy smiled. Kreamer said he would place both items in a safe deposit box at QUEENSTOWN BANK tomorrow morning. Browne urged Megan to do so and stated for effect, "If this involved the famous Captain Thomas Boyle, there could even be hidden treasure on Kent Island."

Jeter, feigning extreme concern, urged Kreamer to make a copy of the parchment before placing it in the vault. Then they would have a back-up. Since he was so experienced in the field, he could meet Kreamer tomorrow morning to accomplish this with his special equipment. Browne refrained from rolling her eyes as she knew Jeter did not have the proper machines to do this. Kreamer said it was an excellent idea. Jeter grabbed a handful of Christmas cookies, said his goodbyes, and left.

All watched out the door windows as Jeter walked over to down a few at the NO PLACE bar. Tomorrow Tom would take the two items to Jeter's house at 10:00am before "going to the bank." With him would be the bogus, almost duplicate, map and the souvenir compass that Browne brought with her from the University of Maryland bookstore. Her specialist map friend had done an excellent job of forgery. The real items were at the library safe. These imposters served their purpose tonight and would tomorrow also.

Megan, Browne, Kreamer and especially Missy felt the first big tug on their fishing line. They toasted to tomorrow's adventure. Was this man Jeter that dumb or that greedy? Or both? He would reveal himself tomorrow in Dominion.

Chapter Twenty-four

When Horace returned home around midnight, the first thing he did was search high and low for the old compass he swindled from a nice widow at a yard sale years ago. He had told her it was worthless when it wasn't. It was surprisingly close enough to switch tomorrow on an unsuspecting Kreamer. He set up a large copier that he salvaged from a junk heap years ago in Easton. Unbelievably, it still worked.

"How stupid are these idiot people!" he kept repeating out loud. By noon tomorrow he'd have a copy of the portion of the map he was missing and the compass found by some dock builder. By News Years Day, if he figured out the correct compass readings, he would be lugging his backhoe for the last time. He went to bed, then snored loudly as he dreamt about treasure scenes from *Pirates of the Caribbean*.

Missy drove home and prepared all the ingredients on her kitchen table for her black walnut Christmas cakes. Tomorrow she would bake. She slid into bed dreaming of holiday smoked rockfish...in particular, one big smoked rockfish.

Chapter Twenty-five

Kreamer was listening to Manheim Steamroller's Christmas songs as he pulled into Dominion on the 22nd and found Jeter's house by 9:55am. He noticed an old, grey shed in back with a backhoe inside. Stacks of rusted junk were thrown about the yard.

Within fifteen minutes, Jeter made the copy and had switched the compass when he asked Tom to plug in the extension cord in the next room, which Kreamer willingly did. The President smiled as he drove down Little Creek Road. By the time he turned left on to Dominion Road, he was laughing as he looked at the bogus compass Jeter had substituted. Now he was certain Jeter was the one involved. He thought how greed led to blindness and outright stupidity. He called Missy on his cell.

Jeter cleared the kitchen table, brought out his side of the map, and began to pour over the co-ordinates on the bottom left of the copied portion. Unfortunately for him, these were Kam Browne's and not Captain Boyle's. Not knowing Jeter had the other piece of the map, Browne had pinpointed a location that would lead Jeter directly to a lot north at Love Point.

Chapter Twenty-Six

Horace spent the entire afternoon drinking beer and studying the two map sections. No matter how much he tried, Jeter could not see how the bearing directions took him south past Matapeake. All these years of digging may have been in vein. He had read of pirate distractions where location points were bogus markings that lead the unsuspecting on wild goose chases. He convinced himself that Captain Boyle must have created his southern side of the map to throw others off. It did not make any sense, but Jeter was beyond logic at this point. He concentrated only on the new copy now.

He would do a dry run tomorrow morning on the 23rd. Destiny could be his somewhere near Love Point. He went out to the shed and filled the backhoe with diesel. What a wonderful Christmas gift the Grinch would have by tomorrow evening. He had no clue.

Chapter Twenty-Seven

Two young men, nephews of Tom Kreamer, sat on an old abandoned dirt road in their used, black Grand Cherokee. It was evening on the 22nd, the day Kreamer and Jeter met, and it was now extremely cold. The wind made the jeep sway. Their uncle would pay them $50.00 each to park here from 8:00pm to 5:00am with one mission; call him if anyone drove down Pier Road on Love Point in a dark pick-up, hauling a backhoe. Tom told them no details but instructed them not to confront anyone; just keep headlights off and call him immediately. It involved stealing property from the KIHS.

The nephews thought their uncle a bit crazy, but this was easy holiday money. Patrick and Kyle munched on Subway sandwiches and quizzed each other on Trivial Pursuit questions. At family gatherings their team always lost. Not this Christmas! Then they listened to I-Tune downloads until they took turns sleeping. No one showed that night except a few hungry deer. The *Rolling Stones* had even scared them away.

Their uncle Tom met them early for breakfast at CRACKER BARREL, paid them, and asked if they could do it for one more evening. They pressed for reasons. Tom repeated his story that someone was potentially stealing artifacts from the KIHS, and they wanted to catch him red-handed. Although still skeptical, they consented, since fifty bucks was fifty bucks. They would dress warmly as the night of the 23rd was due for temperatures in the 20s.

Chapter Twenty-eight

Missy was disappointed that no fish was caught on the 22nd. She agreed with Tom that one more night was worth it. After that, if any ground was disturbed near Browne's fake final marking at Love Point, they would press Sheriff Costello to confront Jeter anyway. The best scenario, however, was to catch him in the act.

Browne had placed the final "X" within the property lines of the LANGENFELDER COMPANY – not far from where the steamship *Emma Giles* had moored for safety that stormy summer day in 1920.

Jeter moved slowly through Chester, passing the first marker point near the KRAM AND McCARTHY red and white sign, across from CHESAPEAKE OUTDOORS. The next compass reading took him west through the small rotary near Castle Marina. Smoke came from his Ford tailpipe as he drove past an abandoned farmhouse on the right. Horace wondered about that old farmer. If alive today, would he ever think a DUNKIN DONUTS drive-thru would face his corn fields!

The final three markers, if his compass interpretations were right, took him past MR.B's SEAFOOD on State Street, turned him left onto Lowery Street, and then went in a straight line past Kent Island High School directly to Love Point.

Kyle and Patrick, bored to insanity, took turns watching. They heard the truck before they saw the headlights. They cut the music. It was approaching 1:30am, now officially Christmas Eve. They hunched down as an old truck, towing a backhoe, slowly rumbled by the dirt road and their hidden jeep.

Patrick had his uncle on speed-dial, "An old Ford with a backhoe just rode past us. The man got out of his truck with a flashlight and is walking around. What do you want us to do?"

Tom woke up his wife Susan by yelling, "Nothing! Just stay where you are, and we'll be there in thirty minutes. If things get dicey, get out of there and don't stop for anything!"

Patrick and Kyle could clearly see that, about two hundred yards away, the man was unloading his equipment.

Tom called Missy and then Sheriff Costello. He would pick up Missy; she insisted on coming. The Sheriff was not happy with Tom's quick explanation, but said he and a deputy would be on Pier Road in twenty minutes. Tom requested they wait for him. The Sheriff was now responding favorably because Tom threw out the words 'night digger.' He didn't know Jeter was one and the same, but it made sense now.

Chapter Twenty-nine

Some fifty yards past the gated entrance to the LANGENFELDER property (Jeter had dropped the chain easily enough), a very cold man was digging a big hole in earnest. The moon was providing plenty of natural light as Jeter carefully examined each scoop of the backhoe. He was giving up on the first hole and beginning a second one when he noticed in the distance the blue police lights, followed by two other vehicles. The solitary gravel road left Jeter no place to run or hide.

Sheriff Costello asked for identification and had the deputy frisk Jeter. The vapors of Costello's breath were crisp as he said, "Do you work here, Mr. Jeter? No...then you are trespassing on private property and destroying this company's clearly marked boundaries. What are you doing digging at this hour?"

At this moment, Jeter saw Mrs. Biscuit and Tom Kreamer, with two young men, walking toward his truck. He somehow believed the two KIHS members would vouch for his absurd and bazaar actions. He was dead wrong. In desperation, Jeter showed the policemen his map and compass – as if this would justify his presence here. He claimed he was on a historical mission. Missy laughed.

Costello seized the two portions of the map, the fake compass, and showed them to Kreamer and Missy. In harmony they gasped, "The other part of the map!"

Chapter Thirty

Rreamer quietly explained to the officers the plan they had concocted and that Jeter's actions had absolutely nothing to do with the KIHS. The deputy arrested Horace on the spot. The night digger was stunned.

By morning light Kreamer and Costello easily got the LANGENFELDER owner to press charges. Jeter would be held on trespassing, destruction of property and potentially other 'night digger' issues; something he loudly denied.

At the Sheriff's office, Missy was smart enough to have Costello make a quick copy of the southern portion of the map. Kreamer verified that the fake compass was property of the KIHS (he had marked it), and Jeter was also charged with petty robbery.

On Christmas Eve afternoon, Horace Alex Jeter was released on bail, pending a hearing in three days, but his sorties of hunting treasure were over. He demanded his map back and was told it was needed as evidence. Missy placed the copy of Jeter's map in the library safe and notified Megan, Knott, Robinson, and Kam Browne that a big fish had indeed just been hooked. Could they all meet on December 27th at the Stevensville Library?

Christmas, 2013, was somewhat sweeter for some. Missy and her family devoured her black walnut cake in a festive manner. Kreamer toasted the complete map find at his Christmas dinner, "To the KIHS!" Patrick and Kyle received their additional $50.00 each, still unaware what exactly this all meant. They lost again at Trivial Pursuit. Megan, Knott, Robinson, and Browne all celebrated Christmas in their own family traditions of church, turkey stuffed with oysters, eggnog, carols, and brightly wrapped presents. There would be no post Christmas letdown this year. The 27th was going to be an exciting day. However, in Dominion, sadness was very deep for one depressed Grinch.

Chapter Thirty-one

The Queen Anne County Judge was briefed on everything by Tom Kreamer and Sheriff Costello prior to Jeter's hearing on the morning of the 27th. His Honor, Frank George Harrison, was also an amateur historian and took things like this seriously. How dare anyone fool with the heritage of Kent Island!

Jeter pleaded "Not Guilty" to all charges. He was found "Guilty." The sentence Harrison pronounced was a fine of $500.00 that would be levied to pay for any destruction of the LANGENFELDER property. Charges of trespassing and petty theft would be dropped on one condition – Jeter would donate his portion of the map to the KIHS and forgo any claims on future potential discoveries. Kreamer had coached the Judge well. Jeter resented the bind he was in but reluctantly agreed. He was cornered. He left quickly in disgrace, using his credit card to cover the fine. The bailiff handed the real parchment, southern map side, over to Kreamer.

The headline in the local weekly *Update* was written by an aspiring reporter, Shelby Syracuse:
NIGHT DIGGER SCROOGE CAPTURED ON CHRISTMAS EVE!?!

Jeter was finished on Kent Island. Sherriff Costello let it slip that he believed the actions of the mysterious 'Night

Digger' might be over. He was hoping Jeter was one and the same. An unknown source in the Sheriff's office gave chapter and verse to the young reporter concerning, "the diligent investigative work of the KISD and the daring capture of Mr. Horace Jeter on a cold Christmas Eve night..." Missy, Kreamer, and KIHS members would enjoy this slant of the story for years to come. The map, thank God, was referred to only as "an historical artifact." No one needed more Horace Jeters.

Chapter Thirty-two

At 4:00pm on the 27th of December, all the key people involved in the discovery assembled at the Stevensville Library. Kam Browne brought along her friend and colleague, Pamela Ann Hopkins, an historical navigational expert. Professor Hopkins was involved in tracing the famous voyage of Captain John Smith, the first explorer to map the Chesapeake. Her credentials were first class. Browne and Hopkins had met Missy and Kreamer earlier and poured over the now complete map and compass. Hopkins confirmed Browne's initial findings of age and authenticity.

Kreamer placed the compass and map on the center of the conference room table, around which also sat Megan, Knott, and Robinson. Introductions were completed, and Browne asked Hopkins to explain more about the compass. Using the "T.B." and "1813" artifact, she did in detail.

Professor Hopkins demonstrated how the compass needle worked with a sharp pin and then discussed what the 'face card' signified. "Compass cards at first were marked out in 'points' and not 'degrees' as such. Some had as many as thirty-two points, matching the wind directions that sailors would be familiar with at sea. The 'Cardinal Points' were the four main directions of 'North,' 'South,' 'East' and 'West,'" she explained.

Megan asked why this compass had more of a decoration at what appeared to be North. Pamela explained that the North Point, so important to navigation, was often decorated in ornamental fashion. She showed everyone on this hand-held compass what appeared to be a French "Fleur De Lys," the royal symbol of France. She stated that actually this was a highly decorated "T" standing for the Latin word "Tramontana" or "North Wind."

Browne noted that the fake compass that had been used to foil Horace Jeter was not at all like this one. She had made the readings very easy for Jeter to find the location at Love Point. It was not impossible, but would take time and effort to use this 19th century compass and map. There would be certain assumptions that only Captain Boyle knew and trusted by heart that were now a bit blurry to this GPS generation.

Hopkins and Browne congratulated all present and the KIHS for such a momentous discovery. Now it was time for Missy and Kreamer to take over. They had a proposal to offer.

Chapter Thirty-three

Very simply put, Kreamer would have a legal document drawn up that specified that the entire map and compass would eventually be on loan to the KIHS for future research and historical preservation, courtesy of Megan and Knott.

Before anyone else would receive access to the items, any potential treasure findings would be divided equally between Megan, Knott, and any landowner or government involved. If any diggings were to commence, Kreamer would attempt to require the landowner to agree to some arrangement. If that person did not, then Megan and Knott would keep their respective finds separate, and the KIHS would only display Jeter's portion of the map. Kreamer was trying his best to be fair.

Since Professors Browne and Hopkins already knew of the discoveries, the KIHS would hire them to conduct the search on behalf of all involved. Both instantly agreed to work for *gratis* as this project would allow them a once-in-a-lifetime historical opportunity.

Absolutely nothing would be done until all parties agreed. It took Megan and Knott less than three seconds to say "yes." Mack Robinson offered any digging services for free. The three artifacts would be kept in the safe until January when the Professors would begin their analysis in earnest.

Kreamer asked who exactly knew the combination of the safe, and Missy confessed that she was the only one. All agreed to keep it that way. In the strongest terms, Kreamer urged silence from all involved – even though he had already once ignored his own advice!

Boyle's ghost was now moving very fast.

Chapter Thirty-four

The New Year came and went quietly. Kent Island was now a bit dreary. Even the ever-present seagulls looked cold. Professors Browne and Hopkins studied photographic copies of the map for over two weeks before they made some assumptions to use the real compass that Missy provided. Kreamer agreed to accompany them around the island the third frigid week of January, 2014.

The first two days the trio drove around potential starting points on Boyle's map. By day three they settled on a beach in the northern shadow of the Bay Bridge. This appeared to correspond to where Boyle began his notations. It was now part of the Cross Island Trail used by bikers and joggers in nicer weather. Kreamer visualized a wooden long boat coming ashore here and saw how it would have welcomed the Privateer Captain.

The first solid conclusion Browne and Hopkins came to was that Boyle had to have had some previous knowledge of Kent Island topography. The rough drawing of his map had to come from older map sketches or his own charts. There was no possible way he could have explored the entire island by land if, and this was a big "if", this had been a quick visit. Using this assumption, they determined the compass readings that stretched from a beach landing on the Chesapeake Bay to Kent Narrows, west to east, and from Love

Point to Bloody Point, north to south, were true markings to orient the compass user.

Their belief was that Boyle would not have gone too far inland with a ship anchored in the Bay around 1815. He would have had a small crew for rowing purposes. A crafty Captain would not take unnecessary 'eyes' when hiding something. They could easily be wrong, but they had to begin somewhere.

If these assumptions were valid, then Horace Jeter's section of the map with location dots was truly part of an orientation and, in some ways, a mere distraction. Without knowing it, Jeter had been right. Other distant points were also probably scribbled down to foil anyone but Boyle.

Hopkins noted that the first compass point close by involved a large rock located "six hundred paces due east" from the landing area. She and Browne both knew that tidal shifts, hurricanes, and two centuries of storms could now put that rock under water. They decided to scour the area for two hundred yards inland by foot for at least a mile in either direction.

They headed south first and on day one the going was difficult. It did not help that the temperature was in the 20's and the wind at fifteen mph. For five hours they traversed state lands, a senior citizen center, and then stopped when they entered an expanding business complex with paved roads. There was no huge rock.

Day two brought some light snow, so they postponed their search. On day three they began on the beach location site, went in some two hundred yards and headed north. The going was especially hard with deep marshes and some fences blocking their way. Without the discovery of this huge rock they could not proceed to the next compass point.

Fatigue and chills had set in by three o'clock. On two occasions they lost time explaining to land owners that they were checking out properties for environmental reasons. The second owner told them to get off his land and he even released his dogs. They called it a day, met with Kreamer, and informed him of their frustration. He promised to discreetly ask around regarding large rocks in this area. Neither Browne nor Hopkins noticed the old blue pickup that had been following them at a distance when they left Kreamer's house.

Chapter Thirty-five

Mr. Ted Lee and his family were legendary on Kent Island. His father, Lester, was a dear friend of William Warner, author of the renowned book *Beautiful Swimmers*, the definitive work on "watermen, crabs and the Chesapeake Bay." The chapter, "Lester Lee and the Chicken Neckers" is the perfect example of how Kent Island crabbers had made their living. Lester's grandson, Ted Lee, "Snake" to his friends, ran a very successful tree business out of Dominion, but Father Ted and Snake still 'oystered' and fished their beloved waters.

After his conversation with the search team, Tom Kreamer had stopped by Ted Lee's to buy some local oysters for his wife's birthday party that January weekend. Boyle's ghost was stirring…One topic led to another when Tom broached the subject of the huge rock somewhere down near the hiking trail, "You guys ever hear of a big rock down near that way? Thought you might know if there was…"

Without hesitation the hard-working father and son looked at each other and said in one voice, "You mean Indian Rock?"

They explained to a stunned Kreamer that Teddy, as a young boy, had worked summer construction and actually helped excavate the rock. Kreamer was more than shocked. Snake went on to state, "Back then those historical 'nuts'

(Kreamer winced) tried to block its removal but the judge ordered a sort of compromise. We were allowed to move it but had to haul it to the back of the new high school. They wanted to use it as an entrance sign for the school's nick-name 'The Buccaneers.' Guess it had to go some-where...solved problems for both sides. They never found a sponsor for the carving costs so the rock is still behind the football bleachers."

Kreamer asked if Snake could remember the spot where "Indian Rock" first stood.

"You tell me when you want to go, Mr. Kreamer, and I'll show you. It's a parking lot now," he replied.

Chapter Thirty-six

By the first week of January, Horace Jeter had simmered down a bit – but not much. He began to rationalize again that treasure might still be in his grasp. Greed trumped the law and any "stupid judge" in his warped reasoning. So, he took to following Missy some days and Kreamer on others, just to see if anything regarding the map might develop.

There was nothing on the KIHS on-line postings or in the newspapers so something had to be going on under the radar. Besides, he had nothing else to do. His house was up for sale, and he planned to leave Maryland, so why not hope for one more shot at treasure? His scrubby face turned red when he thought of the idiot judge taking his map away from him. "That was MINE!" he growled. His memory never registered back that he had originally stolen it during the Bloody Point digs.

Jeter had been trailing Kreamer that January day the President met with Browne and Hopkins. He recognized Browne through his hunting binoculars and sensed something was happening. He then followed the two women to the KENT MANOR INN. Now his tracking would be easier. As he filled up his pickup at the BP gas station, he resolved to be at the end of Kent Manor Road each and every morning to hunt these ladies like a Chesapeake Bay retriever. Evil persistence was a strong drug. He smiled a satanic smile.

Chapter Thirty-Seven

Young Ted Lee had no idea why an old rock was so important. Snake agreed to meet Tom Kreamer on January 30th at 8:00am at the LOVE POINT DELI. It was a cold twenty-five degrees with no wind. Tom bought coffee for both, and Ted climbed into Tom's SUV. Snake uttered, "This shouldn't take long as now there are paved roads. Back then we had to fight dirt and mud. It was like a marsh back there."

Tom explained that the KIHS had some interest in the location because it was believed that an old US naval officer used that rock as a marker during the War of 1812.

Snake was satisfied with the explanation because he knew many people loved tracing historical things on Kent Island. He told Tom where his first turn was off Love Point Road and then said, "Take a left here at Terrapin Grove and watch the speed bumps. Go around the back of these buildings to the far end of the parking lot." Ted directed Tom to a spot near the woods that was fairly deserted and stated, "Indian Rock was right here, Mr. Kreamer. We had three backhoes to dig it out and two large forklifts to put it on a flatbed. The truck's tires almost burst taking it across the street to the High School."

Kreamer thanked Snake and took him back to his truck. On the way Ted had showed him the abandoned rock at the home of the Buccaneers. Kreamer took ten minutes to examine it. No carvings were visible, just some old painted graffiti urging the locals to 'BEAT EASTON!'

Tom immediately called Browne. She and Hopkins met him half an hour later at the spot Snake had revealed off Terrapin Grove Road. They were more than thrilled that a huge rock really HAD been in this immediate area and that Tom had managed to track its whereabouts so quickly.

Hopkins pulled out the map copies and did some quick calculations. She pointed north, using the compass where the notations mentioned two large oak trees some "three hundred paces" north by northwest of the rock. All three put on boots for the trek through the woods. Hound dog Jeter had followed at a safe distance and parked between two cars in the back lot, far enough away to avoid being detected.

The ground was wet, almost swampy, but the three moved forward as Hopkins held the compass in her gloved left hand. In about five minutes they discovered one extremely large oak tree and the rotted trunk remains of another. Their excitement grew.

"This has to be correct," said Hopkins, as her breath looked like vapors in the cold morning air. "Now we have a sense of what Boyle meant by paces."

She and Browne studied the map again which read, "Fifty-five paces north by north east – rock clusters…'X'." By now Jeter had lost a visual of them but remained on his evil vigil.

The one real and one amateur historian took Hopkins' lead. They spread out when the paces were walked off, using the compass for guidance. It was Browne who almost fell when she stumbled across some rocks. Kreamer cleared the area with his boots and fifteen to twenty rocks, about two feet long each, were uncovered. All three were pumped with adrenaline when Kreamer asked, "What's next? Where to from here?"

Hopkins smiled and said, "No where...this is IT! The notations end HERE!" They stared at each other, spontaneously shook hands, and hugged.

In the distance, looking west to the Bay, the trio could see a large oil tanker heading north toward Baltimore...much like the old majestic clipper ships did in the early 19th century. Was this really the spot the famous Captain Boyle had chosen? Was something really buried here? And who owned the land on which they stood?

Chapter Thirty-eight

Kreamer, Hopkins, and Browne marked a nearby tree with a slight chip in the bark. Hopkins put the coordinates in her pocket GPS and led them due east to see how far they actually were from Love Point Road. They each counted off their steps as they trudged through under-brush and then a farm field to the highway. They put the distance at 320 yards and noted the closest highway marker. They walked the distance south to Terrapin Grove Road, turned right, and headed for their vehicles.

Jeter almost jumped when they actually passed right in front of his pickup. "How in God's name did they come back from <u>that</u> direction?," he wondered.

Horace had been focusing on the woods. The search party was deep in conversation and did not notice the unshaven map villain. Jeter waited until they left and then hurried into the woods at the end of the parking lot. He wandered around for thirty some minutes and then gave up in exasperation as there were no noticeable markers or foot-prints to follow. He drove back to KENT MANOR INN, but the ladies' car was not there. He waited.

Kreamer called Missy and asked her to get in immediate touch with Megan, Knott, and Robinson for dinner that evening at RUSTICO in Stevensville. He knew the owners, Art and Barb D'Elia, well and reserved the private back room. It was his treat. Missy was told enough that she was happily nervous when she made the calls.

For now, Kreamer, Hopkins and Browne decided to beat the chill and have lunch. He took them for some of the island's famous "Half & Half" soup at the KENTMOOR RESTAURANT near his home. He explained that this was a mixture of half Maryland vegetable crab soup and half Maryland cream of crab soup, the restaurant's specialty. When the heaping bowls were served with tasty Westminster Oyster Crackers, the women praised his culinary choice. They discussed next steps and the meeting that evening.

Kreamer then drove to Centreville to check on land ownership rights where the rocks lay. An hour later he was home and took a hot shower. Jeter saw the women's car return to the INN and, after ten minutes, decided to head back to his place in Dominion. Nothing happening now…he would be back tomorrow morning.

Chapter Thirty-nine

"The Magnificent Seven" (Kreamer's corny moniker of himself, Missy, Megan, Knott, Robinson, Browne and Hopkins) ordered appetizers at RUSTICO and waited for the waitress to leave before getting down to business. The poor girl, Babzina, actually thought these people were a really "dud bunch" since they never talked when she entered the private room. Ironically, RUSTICO stood two doors down from the old shop where Jake Muth had purchased his nautical junk back in 1920. It was also catty-corner from the PEACE OF CAKE bakery.

Kreamer summarized the search team's findings and told them of the general location of the rocks. They all looked dumfounded. Hopkins explained their methodology, and Browne confirmed that once the location of the huge rock was ascertained, it was relatively easy. Their assumptions seemed to be correct. No one knew if anything would be discovered, but they were optimistic. The mood became so festive that Mack Robinson, after a few bourbon and waters, wanted to bring in his backhoe and dig tomorrow morning!

"Hold on," interjected Kreamer, "that brings us to the land ownership issue. The people in Centreville were very helpful and it appears the property is owned by an elderly farmer by the name of Keith Dunn. He has farmed this land since the 1970's, and the rock area is definitely part of his land."

Missy piped up, "You mean 'Whitey' Dunn, the old hippy? I've known him for years…he and my deceased husband used to hunt geese every winter on his farm. Haven't talked to him in decades, but he would remember me. Let me be the contact person."

The rest of the dinner was spent creating a game plan for Missy, Hopkins and Browne to approach Dunn the next day. They'd explain that an historical find might be on his property and would request permission to do a slight dig in his woods. It was something to do with the War of 1812 and its bicentennial for Kent Island. They would disturb no farmland.

If he gave approval and they found something, then Kreamer would inform Dunn of this third share scenario and hope he would agree. Missy said he was a fair man and would go along. It was delicate but could work. If nothing was discovered, Whitey would have the thanks of the KIHS and the UNIVERSITY OF MARYLAND team, and they would start another search.

Throughout this discussion, Megan and Knott looked like two people who just won the Mega Millions; it couldn't be helped. Mr. Secrecy Kreamer stressed again 'tight lips' and, as they were leaving, Professor Hopkins returned the real compass and map copies to Missy to lock in the safe. All would be kept informed by Missy and, if everything went well, they would be digging in two days, winter weather permitting.

Chapter Forty

The frosty air the next morning did not keep Missy from meeting Browne and Hopkins for a quick breakfast at RAMS HEAD. Aunt Verna was still there cooking up her famous AM delights. It was now the last day of January.

Jeter had been at his post since 7:00am and followed the two ladies easily when they emerged at 9:00am. He sipped lukewarm coffee, hunkered down in the back parking lot of the tavern. He still had no idea who the other person was with Browne. Missy entered a few minutes later, and he perked up. Something was indeed going down.

Inside it was toasty as, even this early, the fireplace was roaring. Missy informed them that she made contact with Whitey very early that morning, and he agreed to meet them at 10:00am. She said, "He's still living in the past, so I could tell he remembered me. He was curious but said he would be glad to see me again. Let me take the lead and explain in vague terms the '1812' possible connections. I'm sure he remembers Indian Rock. Let's stay away from pirates and treasure. 'Artifacts' is the way to go."

The two cars pulled out of RAMS HEAD at 9:50am, headed toward Love Point Road, and turned right. Jeter had trouble getting out of the parking lot and almost lost them. As the women maneuvered onto Dunn's gravel path, Jeter had to back off as it was a private drive. He found a small area off Love Point Road and parked illegally on the shoulder.

The *Moody Blues* were blaring full blast when Missy knocked for the second time on the old oak door. Dunn, now sporting white hair and a white beard, warmly welcomed Missy with a hug and shook hands with the historians. With his Jerry Garcia profile he just said, "Call me Whitey." He turned off the music. After some banter about the good old days and a few stories about Missy's husband and "his big old shotgun," Dunn allowed them to speak.

As Missy went into vague detail about what the KIHS and the UNIVERSITY OF MARYLAND were looking to investigate, Browne and Hopkins were giving each other 'the eye' as they recognized the strange potted plants around Dunn's kitchen. They knew what *cannabis* was. Some of the growth reached to the ceiling.

Hopkins pointed to the woods where they believed some artifacts from the War of 1812 might be found. Whitey said there was an old access road nearby that they could use for any vehicles. Browne wished they had seen that the other day.

"As long as nobody disturbs my fields, go ahead. I'll be planting the spring crop in about a month and a half," said Whitey.

He was heading up to Vermont tonight to meet up with his old musician buddy, Purple Haze Harrington, for the Woodstock Review Band Festival. He'd be back on February 5th so, "Good luck, ladies. Good hunting."

After profuse thanks to Dunn, the trio drove their cars to Missy's house in Chester and laughed as Browne kept calling them by Whitey's "Dude" and "Hey, man." Missy prepared Irish tea. Whitey was extremely nice, but he had never left the 60's. However, they had his blessing to explore.

Jeter's truck put out heavy exhaust fumes as he waited on Bayside Drive near Missy's house. He could see movement inside through his binoculars. Something, indeed, was going down. He contemplated his next move.

Chapter Forty-one

rowne and Hopkins headed out to Annapolis to buy some sifting squares and special tools used during digs. Jeter followed them until he saw the car heading toward the Bay Bridge. He swerved onto the last exit, turned left, and went to the KENT MANOR INN. When they didn't return after an hour, he left in frustration and went back to Missy's house just in case.

Inside, Missy was on the phone with Kreamer, then Megan and finally, Knott. She asked to speak with Mack Robinson and in strong tones said, "Have your backhoe gassed up for tomorrow morning; it's a go! Everyone will meet on the back parking lot of the High School. Our historians want to check on Indian Rock out of curiosity first. See you at 9:00am."

By 4:00pm Jeter's truck was running low on gas. Nothing was happening here except speeders on Queen Anne's Drive. A few almost nipped his truck. He filled up at the EXXON station in Chester, went to the INN, and discovered the ladies' car now in the parking lot. He drove home angry again. Something told him that tomorrow could be the day – but the day for what? This time, regardless, he would not be denied. He had now determined to go beyond any laws or any semblance of historical preservation. In Jeter's warped mind, anything and everything was now justified.

Chapter Forty-two

The Magnificent Seven were all at the High School on time. February 1st started out in the high 30's, but could warm up, according to the 50% always right weatherman. Megan passed out some PEACE OF CAKE cherry turnovers as everyone watched Browne and Hopkins walk slowly around Indian Rock. Some five minutes later it was show time.

Kreamer drove Missy, Megan and the historians, while Knott climbed into Robinson's large truck, the backhoe in toe. Hopkins would direct them to Dunn's old dirt road and had instructed them to drive very slowly. When the two vehicles veered left, Jeter, in tracking mode, again parked illegally on Love Point Road. He went on foot at some distance behind the backhoe, hiding amidst trees and bushes. His heart raced as he took extreme risks of being discovered. He didn't care.

When the dirt road ended, Hopkins pulled out her GPS and started into the woods. From here it was only about forty yards. Kreamer showed everyone the stones and the marked tree. Missy mused that whatever was buried here was only some forty yards from being cleared and plowed under by Dunn years ago. Robinson unloaded his backhoe and was in position to dig, so he shut off the engine.

Browne and Hopkins gave detailed instructions on how they must be careful with every movement. Knott, Robinson, and Kreamer would gingerly remove the rocks by hand and stack them over by a birch tree. Then the historians would show them how to slowly rake the area yard by yard. Except for Missy, they would take turns and if anything was hit, they were to stop immediately and wait until it was examined.

After forty-five minutes, some small stones, root pieces and old pine cones were tossed to one side. Browne and Hopkins wanted this done by the book but realized that the others desired to move faster. Their concerns were voiced to the other five; Knott and Megan spoke up and said using the backhoe was alright with them.

Mack, the former teacher, was now being lectured by the two professors on "one inch depth," "delicacy of movement," and "slow-motion techniques." He climbed aboard his trusted red machine, lit his pipe, and moved closer into position. All eyes were on the special small shovel he had installed just yesterday.

Jeter watched everything through his hunting binoculars, crouched on one knee behind some holly bushes. Twice he grossly relieved "Mother Nature" against a pine tree. The man was crude.

Chapter Forty-three

Robinson was stopped repeatedly for digging too deep, but eventually seemed to have the proper technique down. The collected dirt was placed in a pile by the rocks, which Hopkins and Browne sifted with their screens. Everyone had the same thought, "Just how deep in 1815 would someone dig?" Assumptions were that Boyle must have had help, but anything beyond five feet was a stretch. Hell, most men were no more than five feet four in those days.

Robinson worked in squares that the historians had roughly marked off. He was told to stop immediately if the shovel dragged. Three times he had to do this, but it was only rocks. By now, Missy and Megan warmed up in Kreamer's SUV. The trees made this area dark and cold.

A little more than four feet down the shovel hesitated again. Mack stopped and lifted the bucket vertically. Knott jumped into the hole and yelled, "I think we got something!"

Megan and Missy came back quickly, as Browne and Hopkins dropped the sifters and asked Knott to please be careful. Robinson moved the shovel arm, cut the engine, and stood next to Kreamer.

Knott dug around a two foot by three foot box that had the composition of hardened pine wood. It had been covered

by some sort of thick canvas that was now almost deterio-
rated by the dirt. The historians jumped into the hole with
a small broom-like instrument. They gently brushed the
top of the rectangle and confirmed what Knott could
already see; it was a chest of some sort! Now everything had
to proceed with extreme caution. Seven hearts, plus one,
were racing...

Chapter Forty-four

What seemed like an hour actually took ten minutes. Robinson and Knott would dig around the box, and then Hopkins and Browne would step in to gingerly clean away the surrounding dirt. They dug past rotting leather hinges on the back and a strange hooked device on the front that was closed by inserting an iron nail through the rough loops.

Every new sweep of the chest brought out Kreamer's camera as he snapped away. The depth of the actual box was no more than a foot. The diggers went past the bottom so the historians could unearth the ground underneath. At last the chest was free.

Megan went back to the SUV and retrieved the roll of heavy plastic that Browne had placed there. Very carefully, Robinson and Knott lifted the wooden box and placed it on the plastic. The historians wrapped it like a Christmas present and taped the plastic completely. The chest was not that heavy as it was lifted from the hole and given to Kreamer.

Like a tailgate party, everyone gathered to observe the plastic object on the SUV back-gate as the sun beamed down. The warmth felt good. This odyssey had begun back around Halloween and now, a little over three months later, it was coming to a very suspenseful ending.

It took Robinson and Knott about ten minutes to refill the dig and replace the stones. Meanwhile, the other five warmed up inside the SUV and discussed where to go to open the chest. Missy excused herself, borrowed Tom's cell phone, and stepped outside to make a call. She had to cancel her canasta lunch date. Megan offered the PEACE OF CAKE, as they were closed today. Good choice...it was close by. Knott agreed as he and Mack finished loading the backhoe. They would follow the others to the bakery. All were beaming with justified excitement.

Chapter Forty-five

About a hundred yards from Love Point Road, another truck was headed directly at Tom's SUV. It was going so fast that the dust behind it kicked up high into the air. At the last second, the unknown driver swerved to block the small path and a man with a rifle pointed it directly at Kreamer. Knott and Robinson got out to see what was happening and were told to put their hands up. By now everyone, even Hopkins by instinct, knew this was Horace Jeter.

When Tom and Missy rolled down their windows and tried to speak, Jeter yelled, "Everyone shut up! Kreamer, release the back door-latch – now! Everybody just stay calm; all I want is what is rightfully MINE."

He pointed the rifle at Robinson's chest and demanded that he and Knott back up.

Missy, in her soft voice said, "You'll never get away with this. Everyone has seen you, Mr. Jeter."

He answered by shooting out the SUV's and Mack's front tires, reloading very quickly. He then collected cell phones and tossed them into the woods. Jeter hoisted up the plastic wrapped chest on his shoulder and put it in his truck's passenger side. He sneered, "No one try to follow me, or I'll destroy the chest, so help me God! So back off you losers; thanks for doing the dirty work."

Chapter Forty-six

As Jeter maneuvered his truck around, he checked the rearview mirror to make sure no one followed on foot. He smiled at the object on his front seat and tapped it gently. "You're mine now," he mused.

The Magnificent Seven went from euphoria to depression in less than a minute. How did this guy track us? How did he know where we'd be today? Can he really get away with this? What do we do now?

All were morose and angry except Missy. For some reason she just smiled and said, "He's going nowhere. Sheriff Costello and his men are waiting at the end of the road. I called him after I noticed bright sun reflections coming out of the woods about fifty yards from our dig. Warming up in the SUV gave me time to figure this out. At first, I thought it might be a hunter, but that made no sense. Did not want to alarm all of you in case I was wrong, but I really didn't think Jeter would be so bold. Guess his kind never gives up. Saw his pickup parked by my house the other day and noticed the same binocular reflections bouncing off my walls. He was tracking us for sure. When I borrowed Tom's cell phone, I called the Sheriff to be ready on Love Point Road just as a precaution. What a foolish man!"

The others looked at Missy with their mouths wide open. Knott said she was better than that lady Jessica Fletcher on *Murder She Wrote!*

At the end of the dirt trail, three policemen aimed their own rifles at the windshield of the old Ford pickup. Jeter's smile melted into a string of curses. He slammed on the brakes, got out, and raised his hands to the sky. Costello clasped on the cuffs and promised the Night Digger guaranteed jail time, as the Miranda Rights were read. This time it was armed robbery and a whole lot more.

Chapter Forty-Seven

ater that same year, September 14, 2014, a reception was being held in the newly constructed Visitors' Center at Fort McHenry in Baltimore. Today would commemorate the exact 200th anniversary that Baltimoreans and their countrymen would celebrate as the turning point in the War of 1812. It was the first time the British would be repulsed on such a scale in their efforts to crush this upstart former colony.

For two long days in September, 1814, their finest Limey warships threw everything they had at the Fort. The bombing was almost incessant. American soldiers, sailors and ordinary citizens resisted the British military advance from North Point and stopped their troops at Hampstead Hill. Attempted landings by the British had also been repulsed when they tried to outflank Fort McHenry.

Finally, on the historic morning of the 14th, the Commander of the Star Fort, Major George Armistead, saw the unbelievable. The British fleet hoisted sail and turned back toward Chesapeake Bay. They had given up! He instructed his men to take down the smaller 'Storm Flag' with its fifteen stars and stripes and hoist up the biggest United States flag anyone had even seen. Baltimoreans were still in control!

Mary Pickersgill's 'Garrison Flag' was 30 feet by 42 feet. Armistead wanted the frustrated and retreating British to

Anna Formica - Kent Island High School *(Class of 2012)*

have absolutely no doubt whom they lost to on this beautiful September morning. This was the flag that a lawyer named Francis Scott Key saw as he watched from the U.S. truce ship *President*, waiting for the release of his captured client from the British. It inspired him to craft a poem that he later finished at Baltimore's INDIAN QUEEN TAVERN, which he called: "The Defense of Fort McHenry." Americans now call it their National Anthem.

A newspaper from Boston was quoted by the Baltimore *Niles Weekly Register* on October 1, 1814, "Rejoice ye people of America! Inhabitants of Philadelphia, New York and Boston rejoice! Baltimore has nobly fought your battles! Thank God, and thank the people of Baltimore!"

Two hundred years later, to the day, gathered around one of the newest exhibits at Fort McHenry, was the Magnificent Seven and Whitey Dunn. He and Knott even wore suits and ties. Behind a special glass display case hung the original historic and beautiful painting of "The Pride of Baltimore" by the renowned artist Frank Nicolette. Captain Thomas Boyle's ghost was relishing this perfect rendition of his beloved *Chasseur* under sail.

Inside the glass case, on fine blue velvet, rested an exquisite gold crown adorned with rubies and emeralds. It was in pristine condition. The brass plaque beneath it read:

BRITISH CROWN SEIZED BY CAPTAIN THOMAS BOYLE DURING WAR OF 1812 WHEN HIS SHIP *CHAUSSER* CAPTURED THE BRITISH BRIG *MARQUIS OF CORNWALLIS* OFF THE IRISH COAST IN 1814.

DISCOVERED ON KENT ISLAND, MARYLAND IN 2014. DONATED TO THE FORT McHENRY HISTORICAL SITE IN HONOR OF CAPTAIN THOMAS BOYLE AND ALL WAR OF 1812 AMERICAN PRIVATEERS.

BEQUEATHED BY DEVOTED PATRIOTS OF KENT ISLAND.

A photographer had just snapped a picture of the group. Kreamer requested numerous copies. Each member of the Kent Island delegation had his or her personal reflections that led to this day. God willing, some would be telling their grandchildren's children this strange tale.

"THE CHASSEUR" WAR OF 1812

Taylor Day - Kent Island High School *(Class of 2012)*

Chapter Forty-eight

The plastic covered chest had been returned immediately to the group by Sheriff Costello. It was unwrapped at the PEACE OF CAKE back on the morning of February 1, 2014. The wooden cover was surprisingly easy to open. Hopkins and Browne removed an object wrapped in sail cloth that was faded but fairly intact. Inside was the beautiful crown and a simple handwritten note penned by Captain Boyle on rough parchment. It read, "Seized by American Vessel *Chausser* from British ship *Marquis of Cornwallis*. Complete surrender offered on August 26th off the coast of Ireland. The year of our Lord, 1814."

Everyone in the group took turns holding the crown. Each was mesmerized. It was agreed that Hopkins and Browne should take it for further quiet study and report back as quickly as possible. No one else would be informed of the find. Even Kreamer agreed that no publications would go out from the KIHS.

On February 17th the historians met everyone, including Dunn, for lunch in the familiar backroom of RUSTICO in Stevensville. Kreamer and Missy had visited Dunn and told him of the discovery. They had explained the agreement with Megan and Knott and promised Dunn that he would have a definite say in the matter. He agreed.

Browne and Hopkins began by stating that they were able to confirm the existence and capture of the *Marquis of Cornwallis* by Boyle. As of this time, nothing was discovered regarding the actual crown. Traditional markings of the maker were not anywhere on the object, and computer searches of a lost crown during this period were producing nothing. Was this destined for the Court of crazy King George III or his regent, George IV? Much more research was needed and, even then, they might never know. They reported that the crown was made of fourteen karat gold, and the jewels were indeed authentic. Dunn could not take his eyes off of the color photographs of the crown spread out on the table.

For the historians, the most important find was the note from Boyle. It confirmed that the map sections were indeed in his handwriting and, most importantly, that Boyle had landed on Kent Island. They admitted their natural prejudice, but thought the crown belonged in an appropriate American museum. This was history at its finest, and all should be allowed to view it. They had a specific recommendation but knew this was not their call to make. Everyone started eating their salads, and there was a strange quiet in the room.

Chapter Forty-nine

The silence did not last long. One by one, everyone involved in the find had said their thoughts in turn, beginning with Missy at the far end of the table,

"I am thrilled for Kent Island and the KIHS. It would be a shame to see someone purchase a piece of history and not allow others to enjoy it. While it's not really up to me, it belongs in a museum."

Kreamer and Robinson said the same thing in different ways. They sided with the unofficial dean of Kent Island history. Then all eyes went to Megan, who stated, "I have no idea what the value of such a crown is, but I know it is priceless to our Island and part of American history. Do our historian friends know why Boyle would not have included this in his other captured property? This had to be worth a lot – even back then."

Browne, well-versed in the ways of pirates and privateers, said it was a great question. She stated her theory, "Most of the items seized back then were standard fare in the War of 1812: timber, guns and ammunition, wine, clothing, food products, and, of course, the ships themselves. The amounts of coinage and 'treasure' were usually rare. What would Captain Boyle do with a crown – especially if it were meant for the Royal Family in England? My theory is that Boyle was smart to hide it and then wait to see what he should or could do later when things cooled down. A crown could be toxic in war time...total embarrassment for the British and cause for long-term issues. Maybe it could be used in the future for leverage by the Americans? For some reason, Boyle was not going to make this part of the divided spoils. Or was it the pirate in him? Unless we discover more reference to a particular 'missing crown' from that period, we may never know. However, what is written in the man's own hand is that it was taken from a British Brig. What is even more fascinating to us is why did the good Captain never return to claim it?"

Megan was satisfied and simply said, "It belongs in a museum."

Next to speak was Knott. "From a cracker tin to a crown; I have quite a story to tell my grandkids! Anyone willing to buy something of history like this is just scum like that guy Jeter. I vote for the museum idea."

Mack Robinson was very proud of his friend and gave a thumbs up in his direction.

There was dead silence as all stared at Whitey Dunn. After all of Kreamer's explanations to him, the crown was still found on his property. Legally it was his. Kreamer knew that Dunn had the upper hand if they ever had to go to court. Not even the government, with its far-reaching tentacles, could claim that a privateers' goods were not private property. Just what would Whitey decide to do? The air was tense in the back room of RUSTICO. Poor Babzina, the waitress, thought these same 'dud' people had come from a funeral this time.

Chapter Fifty

"**A**nyone know the actual value of this crown in today's market?" Whitey asked.

Browne and Hopkins looked at each other, and Kreamer took a deep breath. Browne responded, "We asked fellow researchers in a hypothetical way last week. They put the non-historical value today at about $280,000 worth of gold and gems. The historical provenance, the connection to Boyle and the British, makes it priceless."

After a very long pause that nearly killed poor Kreamer, Whitey said, "$280,000 could buy a lot of farm equipment and things. God knows how long it would take me to make THAT much money! But I tell you what; I have a deal to make with all of you. Speaking of pirates, it's what I believe they called a 'parley'."

Everyone stared at old Whitey and did a double-take. Kreamer was visibly sweating.

"If the town of Stevensville and Queen Anne's County let me build my new barn without any of those 'environmental wacko' hassles and restrictions, I vote for a museum too! Can you, Mr. Kreamer, set up a 'parley' for me?"

After dobbing the sweat from his brow with a napkin, Kreamer asked that everyone pretend that they did not hear the last part of Mr. Dunn's statement. He assured Whitey that he would do everything in his power to intervene on his behalf with the understanding members of the zoning commission – IF this were at all possible. Most were members of the KIHS. He could make no promises but felt that they would gladly help one of Kent Island's regular farmers through any mine field regulations.

So everyone toasted the final decision and Hopkins laughed really hard when Browne whispered, "Wonder just what Whitey will be growing in that new barn?"

Epilogue

On October 30, 2014, Missy received a call from Megan Shockley, asking her to come and visit her at the PEACE OF CAKE. Megan had a surprise for her. Missy would be there in twenty minutes.

By now, the story of "Boyle's Treasure" was spread across all of Kent Island and beyond. Thanks to President Kreamer and Missy, it was cause for continuous celebration – especially at the crowded "Kent Island Days" that May. Kreamer got his wish, and there were articles in every major newspaper and noted magazines like the *Smithsonian*. A renewed sense of historical pride was everywhere on the Island.

At local taverns, strangers would buy Knott and Whitey Dunn free drinks when they recognized them. Megan had more and more customers ask if this was *the* bakery where the "treasure hunt" started. Mack Robinson let everyone know that it was *his* company that dug up the buried crown. He even went back to Kent Island High School and gave lectures on the find.

Hopkins and Browne, on a different stage, were writing a collaborative book on this unbelievable Maryland discovery. They often wondered what their British counterparts would think of an 1814 English crown now residing in perpetuity at Baltimore's Fort McHenry!

As Missy gingerly negotiated the old wooden steps at PEACE OF CAKE, she saw the small shop was crowded. Megan and staff were all dressed as 19th Century pirates and Knott, Mack, Whitey, and Kreamer were also there – invited by Megan who announced, "We wanted you at PEACE OF CAKE, Mrs. Biscuit, for the official dedication. One year ago today everything got started when I fell off the stepladder. Will you do us the honor of cutting our newest creation:

CAPTAIN BOYLE'S BLACK PIRATE WALNUT CAKE!

We hope you recognize the recipe."

THE END

Acknowledgements

First of all, thanks are due to the wonderful people of Kent Island whose proud history and determined spirit helped create this work. The Kent Island Heritage Society continues to kindle this justified pride.

Any possible inaccuracies or unintentional mistakes are solely my responsibility.

I am indebted to the many friends and colleagues who offered suggestions and took the time to read and edit the initial manuscripts. They were all very patient and encouraging, but none more than my friends, Professor Mark McComas of Stevensville, Professor Kay Schuyler of Baltimore, and my godmother, Edith Muth of Towson.

Special thanks, also, to Scott Sheads, Ranger, Fort McHenry National Monument & Historic Shrine for his historical input. He is indeed a wealth of knowledge.

Lastly, all the artwork has been expertly created by some very talented students of our Kent Island High School. Kudos goes to them. Go Buccaneers!

Selected Bibliography

Eshelman, Ralph E.; Sheads, Scott S.
and Donald R. Hickey. *The War of
1812 in the Chesapeake.*
Baltimore, Maryland: The Johns
Hopkins University Press, 2010.

Freedman, Janet. *Kent Island (The
Land That Once Was Eden).*
Baltimore, Maryland: Maryland
Historical Society, 2002.

Holly, David C. *Steamboat on the
Chesapeake.* Centreville,
Maryland: Tidewater Publishers,
1987.

Holly, David C. *Chesapeake Steamboats
(Vanished Fleet).* Centreville,
Md.: Tidewater Publishers, 1994.

Hoxter, Nick. *Growing Up on Kent
Island.* Grasonville, Maryland:
Wm. N. Hoxter, Jr. and MRH
Publishing LLC, 2000 Edition.

Lewis, Brent. *Remembering Kent Island (Stories From The Chesapeake).* Charleston, South Carolina: The History Press, 2009.

Sheeds, Scott and Jerome Bird. *Privateers From The Chesapeake.* Baltimore, Md.: The National Park Service, 2001.

Warner, William W. *Beautiful Swimmers.* Boston-Toronto: Little, Brown and Company, 1976.

CPSIA information can be obtained at www.ICGtesting.com
Printed in the USA
BVOW04s2220180714

359370BV00001B/161/P